MAX
Counts His Chickens

1 6 4 3
8 2 7
9 5 10

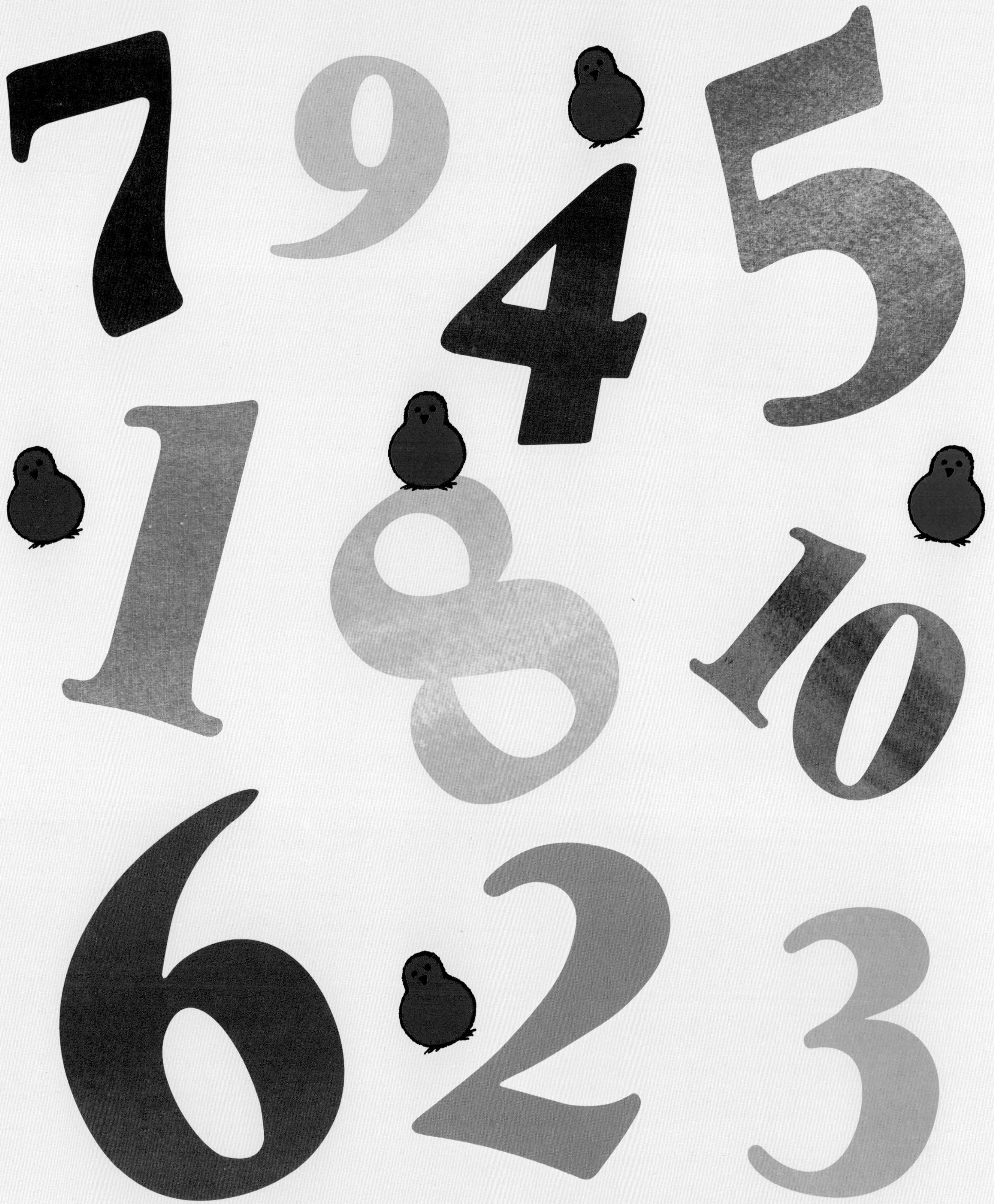
7
9
4
5
1
8
10
6
2
3

MAX
Counts His Chickens

ROSEMARY WELLS

PUFFIN BOOKS

It was Easter morning.

The Easter Bunny hid ten hot-pink marshmallow chicks all over the house.

"That should be plenty!" said the Easter Bunny.

"Finders keepers, Max!" said Max's sister Ruby.

"Finders keepers!" said Max.

Ruby found chick one under her pillow.
"My chick is too beautiful to eat, Max!"
said Ruby.

There was another chick in Ruby's dollhouse.
"That makes two!" said Ruby. "Let's look in the
bathroom, Max."

3

"Here's number three on the tub taps!" said Ruby.
Max looked in the bath-bead bottle.
There were no chicks.

"There's one in the soap dish!" said Ruby.

"Now I have four!"

There were no chicks in the toothpaste tube.

5

Ruby was sure there were chicks in the
dining room.
"Wow, Max!" said Ruby. "That makes five!"

But Max had no luck in the dining room.
"I'll bet there are chicks in the living room,
Max," said Ruby.

6

"Bull's-eye!" said Ruby. "Six chicks!
Look at all my beautiful chicks!"

There were no chicks hiding in the cushions for Max.
"Your chicks are probably in the kitchen, Max,"
said Ruby.

Ruby peeked into the mixing bowl.

"Seven!" said Ruby.

There were no chicks in the coffee can.

Ruby opened the oven.

"Eight!" said Ruby.

There were no chicks in the
Healthy-Os or the Wispie Crisps.

"Look, look, Max! One in the breadbox!"
said Ruby. "That makes nine!"

"Chick! Chick! Chick!" said Max.
But no chick was hiding in the orange juice.

Ruby looked on the pantry shelf.
"Ten hot-pink chicks!" shouted Ruby.
"All mine!"

Suddenly Grandma came in.
"Oh, dear!" said Grandma. "I'd better
make a telephone call!"

The Easter Bunny answered the telephone.
"Oh, no!" said the Easter Bunny. "I'll come
right away!"

Pop! Pop! Pop! Pop! Pop! Pop! Pop! Pop! Pop! Pop!
went the mail slot.
All of Max's marshmallow chicks came through.

"One, three, ten, two, six, four, seven, eight, nine, five!" said Max. "All mine!"

To Russell, Cynthia, and Natasha

PUFFIN BOOKS
Published by the Penguin Group
Penguin Young Readers Group, 345 Hudson Street, New York, New York 10014, U.S.A.
Penguin Group (Canada), 90 Eglinton Avenue East, Suite 700, Toronto, Ontario,
Canada M4P 2Y3 (a division of Pearson Penguin Canada Inc.)
Penguin Books Ltd, 80 Strand, London WC2R 0RL, England
Penguin Ireland, 25 St Stephen's Green, Dublin 2, Ireland
(a division of Penguin Books Ltd)
Penguin Group (Australia), 250 Camberwell Road, Camberwell, Victoria 3124, Australia
(a division of Pearson Australia Group Pty Ltd)
Penguin Books India Pvt Ltd, 11 Community Centre, Panchsheel Park,
New Delhi - 110 017, India
Penguin Group (NZ), 67 Apollo Drive, Rosedale, North Shore 0632, New Zealand
(a division of Pearson New Zealand Ltd)
Penguin Books (South Africa) (Pty) Ltd, 24 Sturdee Avenue, Rosebank, Johannesburg 2196, South Africa

Registered Offices: Penguin Books Ltd, 80 Strand, London WC2R 0RL, England

First published in the United States of America by Viking, a division of Penguin Young Readers Group, 2007
Published by Puffin Books, a division of Penguin Young Readers Group, 2009

5 7 9 10 8 6 4

LIBRARY OF CONGRESS CATALOGING-IN-PUBLICATION DATA IS AVAILABLE
ISBN: 978-0-670-06222-5 (hc)

Text set in Minister.

Puffin Books ISBN 978-0-14-241274-9

Printed in the United States of America

7 9 4 5 1 8 10 6 2 3